"Now we're *really* in trouble," Timothy said. "For some crazy reason, somebody put a key in an Easter egg. Then that person put the egg up high on the grown-ups' bookcase. Usually putting stuff up high means kids aren't supposed to mess with it."

Titus said slowly, "So, if we rehide the egg like Mrs. Hendricks told us to, we could get in trouble with the person who put it there in the first place."

"Bingo," said Timothy.

Sarah-Jane said, "But if we *don't* rehide the egg, we could get in trouble with Mrs. Hendricks."

"Double bingo," said Timothy.

"So now what do we do?" asked Titus.

THE MYSTERY OF THE
HIDDEN
EGG

Elspeth Campbell Murphy
Illustrated by Chris Wold Dyrud

Chariot Books™
David C. Cook Publishing Co.

A Wise Owl Book
Published by Chariot Books™,
an imprint of David C. Cook Publishing Co.
David C. Cook Publishing Co., Elgin, Illinois 60120
David C. Cook Publishing Co., Weston, Ontario

THE MYSTERY OF THE HIDDEN EGG
© 1991 by Elspeth Campbell Murphy for text and Chris Wold Dyrud
for illustrations

Cover design by Stephen D. Smith
First Printing, 1991
Printed in the United States of America
95 94 93 92 91 5 4 3 2 1

Library of Congress Cataloging-in-Publication Data
Murphy, Elspeth Campbell.
    The mystery of the hidden egg / Elspeth Campbell Murphy;
illustrated by Chris Wold Dyrud.
        p. cm.—(Beatitudes mysteries)
    "A Wise owl book"—T.p. verso.
    Summary: Timothy and his two cousins learn the meaning of the
Beatitude "Blessed are the poor in spirit for theirs is the kingdom of
heaven," as they try to solve the mystery of a key hidden inside an
Easter egg.
    ISBN 1-55513-915-9
    [1. Beatitudes—Fiction. 2. Cousins—Fiction. 3. Mystery and
detective stories.] I. Dyrud, Chris Wold, ill. II. Title. III. Series:
Murphy, Elspeth Campbell. Beatitudes mysteries.
PZ7.M95315Myce   1991
[Fic]—dc20   89-29863
                                                              CIP
                                                              AC

CONTENTS

"Blessed are the poor in spirit,
for theirs is the kingdom of heaven."
Matthew 5:3 (NIV)

1
A SECOND CHANCE

Timothy Dawson and his cousins, Sarah-Jane Cooper and Titus McKay, were getting a second chance.

"Neat-O!" said Timothy.

"So cool!" said Sarah-Jane.

"EX-cellent!" said Titus.

The person giving them the second chance was the same person who had given them the first chance. Her name was Mrs. Hendricks, and she was the librarian in the preschool room.

The Greenwood Public Library, where Timothy went all the time, had two children's rooms. The first room was for the little kids. And the second room was for the big kids.

Timothy belonged to the big kids' room, of course. But whenever he was at the library, he stopped by to see Mrs. Hendricks in the little kids' room. She helped him pick out books to read to his baby sister, Priscilla.

Mrs. Hendricks and Timothy had been friends ever since he was a baby himself. That was why she had given him a special job to do last year—hiding eggs for the Annual Preschool Easter Egg Hunt.

Timothy had brought his cousins along to help last year, too. And the three of them had worked really hard.

But they had messed up.

The problem wasn't that they had not hidden the eggs well enough. The problem was that they had hidden them *too* well.

They had hidden the eggs so well that none of the preschoolers could find any. . . . And then all the little kids had started crying. . . . So the cousins had had to help hunt for their own eggs. . . . But no one could find the last one . . . at least not until a l-o-n-g time later . . . when the SMELL finally gave it away. . . .

The cousins hadn't expected to get a second chance after *that* fiasco!

But here it was the Saturday before Easter again. The library was gaily decorated with ribbons and lilies. And here was Mrs. Hendricks, handing each of them a big basket, full of brightly colored eggs.

"It's not that we don't trust you," she said. "But we decided to go with—um—*plastic* eggs this year. No offense."

But the cousins didn't even think about being offended. They were just glad to be getting a second chance.

Timothy said, "Don't worry, Mrs. Hendricks. We won't blow it this time. We won't make it too hard." Then he paused. "But we shouldn't make it too easy, either. Right? Because even preschoolers don't like stuff that's too cinchy."

"That's right," Mrs. Hendricks agreed. "The trick is to stoop down a little so you're at their eye level. It's OK to hide the eggs behind things. Just be sure a little bit is peeping out—and that the kids can reach them."

"We'll make it just the right amount of hard," said Sarah-Jane happily.

"You can depend on the T.C.D.C.," said Titus.

"Oh, I'm sure I can," said Mrs. Hendricks. She gave the cousins a warm smile and turned to her desk. Then right away she turned back with a puzzled look on her face. "What's a 'teesy-deesy'?"

The cousins laughed. It was a question they had heard before—a lot.

"It's letters," explained Timothy.

"Capital T.

Capital C.

Capital D.

Capital C.

It stands for the Three Cousins Detective Club."

"Well, I'm glad I have detectives to do the job of hiding Easter eggs," Mrs. Hendricks said. "But I'm afraid it's not the most exciting job in the world. After all, nothing mysterious ever happens around here."

2
A JOB WELL DONE

The cousins had the preschool room all to themselves. Mrs. Hendricks had stepped out to another part of the library. And a sign by the door told people that the preschool room wouldn't be open for business until after the party.

"OK," said Timothy. "We'll start off the way we did last year. First we'll divide the room into three sections. Then we'll each take a different part. Except *this* year—let's not blow it."

"Right," said Sarah-Jane. "We won't make it too hard for them."

"Right," said Titus. "But not too easy, either."

So they split up and got to work.

But hiding the eggs—so that the hunt would

be just the right amount of hard—was not the easiest thing in the world to do.

Timothy kept thinking up all these incredibly smart places to hide the eggs. Places where *he* would have looked if he were the hunter. But then he reminded himself that preschoolers would never think of looking in those places.

So next he tried just sort of scattering a few eggs around on the floor. But that was no good, either. He knew even his baby sister could find them in half a second.

Timothy gathered up the eggs and started

over. He scrunched down so that he was about the size of a little kid. Pretty soon he saw good places to hide the eggs where the preschoolers could reach them.

When Timothy was done, his legs were achy from scrunching. But he felt happy and satisfied at a job well done.

"Finished!" he announced to his cousins.

"Finished!" replied Titus.

"Finished!" cried Sarah-Jane.

They went to tell Mrs. Hendricks they were finished.

Then they didn't have anything to do until time to help with the party. So they went down the hall to the exhibit room to see a display called *World of Eggs*. They didn't think it would be all that interesting.

But they were wrong.

The exhibit room was filled with the most fabulous, beautiful Easter eggs the cousins had ever seen. For a moment all they could do was stand there and stare.

"So cool," murmured Sarah-Jane.

"Neat-O," agreed Timothy.

"EX-cellent," said Titus. "I mean—EGGS-cellent."

Timothy and Sarah-Jane just looked at him and groaned.

The eggs were so special that they were kept locked up in glass display cases. Also, the security guard came in to check on things. *L. Johnson,* it said on her little, brass name tag. (The cousins always noticed little things like that.)

Because they liked to notice little things, Timothy, Titus, and Sarah-Jane just about went crazy with the eggs. They dashed from case to case, each one trying to get the others to come and look.

"Hey, you guys! Come here. Look at *this* one."

"No, no. Over here. Ooo! Look at *this* one."

"Oh, wow! Look what I found. Look at *this* one."

Then somehow they all met up at the last display table—number seven. And they realized that they hadn't seen *anything* yet.

This case was filled with the most gorgeous

14

eggs they had ever seen. Each egg was covered with tiny, complicated designs. And the eggs were dyed deep, rich colors—yellow, green, blue, orange, red, and black. All the eggs in the case looked like they belonged together. But still, no two were alike. Each one was different and special. In that way, they reminded Timothy of snowflakes.

The sign said *Ukrainian Pysanky.*

"Well, here are some people I know," said a friendly voice behind them.

3
ANNA'S EASTER EGGS

The cousins looked up and were delighted to see Timothy's pastor, Mr. Parry.

"Isn't this wonderful?" he asked, looking all around. "I wouldn't have missed this for anything. I used to be something of an egger myself, you know."

"A *what*?!" asked Timothy, laughing.

Pastor Parry laughed, too. "An egger. An *egger* is someone whose hobby is decorating eggs."

Sarah-Jane frowned thoughtfully. "But that wouldn't be such a good hobby to have. You could only do it at Easter time."

"Oh, no," said Pastor Parry. "Eggers work very happily on their eggs all year round. They decorate eggs for all occasions. But I agree with you. Eggs seem especially right for Easter. People have always associated eggs with springtime and new life. But Christians took the egg as their own special symbol of Easter. That's because the shell reminded them of Jesus' tomb. And the idea of new life reminded them of His Resurrection."

Sarah-Jane pointed to the beautiful eggs in Display Case 7. "Did you ever make Easter eggs like these?" she asked.

"No," said Pastor Parry. "These eggs take an incredible amount of skill and patience and dedication. This is a Ukrainian folk art. There's a part of the Soviet Union called the Ukraine. And people who come from that part of the world are called Ukrainians. Ukrainian women have passed the instructions for making these eggs from mother to daughter. I know one of the ladies—Anna—who did most of these. She's a lovely person."

Titus said, "I sure wouldn't want to go to all that trouble. Because how would you feel if someone cracked the egg and ate it?"

But Pastor Parry said, "These eggs are never

meant to be eaten. They're given as gifts. The giver hands the egg to a friend and says, 'Christ is risen.' And the friend accepts the egg and says, 'He is risen indeed.' An egg decorated like this is called a *pysanka*. People keep *pysanky* and treasure them from year to year."

"For *years*?" asked Timothy. "How come the egg doesn't smell?" (He was remembering the long-lost egg from last year's preschool hunt.)

Pastor Parry explained. "*Pysanky* are decorated raw. Eventually the inside of a raw egg just dries up. The egg won't smell as long as there are absolutely no cracks in it."

Titus said, "Or, you could blow out the inside and just decorate the shell."

"Yes," said Pastor Parry. "You could do that, too."

The cousins loved it when grown-ups talked to them like this.

"How do the ladies get the decorations on the eggs?" asked Sarah-Jane.

Pastor Parry said, "They draw the designs with warm wax. Then they dip the eggs in dye.

The dye won't stick where the wax is. When they take the wax off, they have a white design. Many of the designs have special meanings. For example, do you see those bands going all around the egg? You can't tell where the band begins or where it ends. So it stands for eternal life."

Sarah-Jane looked at the beautiful eggs and sighed. "Anna must be so proud of these."

"Yes," said Pastor Parry. "Anna takes a great deal of pride in her work. But she's not a proud person. If you know what I mean."

The cousins nodded.

Sarah-Jane said, "You mean she's not stuck-up. She doesn't think she's better than everybody else just because she can do something special."

Pastor Parry said, "That's it exactly. In fact, whenever I hear the first Beatitude, I think of people like Anna. 'Blessed are the poor in spirit.' That doesn't mean they're poor because they don't have enough money. To be poor in spirit means to know that everything we have and everything we are comes from God. It

means that we are continually thankful to Him. For Anna, making these beautiful eggs is a real act of worship."

Timothy said, "But I thought worshiping God was something we do at church on Sunday."

"Oh, it is," agreed Pastor Parry. "But we can worship God by everything we do if we do it as a kind of present for Him. In fact, before a Ukrainian woman begins work on a *pysanka* egg, she says a little prayer: 'God, help me!' "

"I can see why!" exclaimed Timothy.

He looked again at the tiny, complicated decorations. The plastic eggs they had hidden in the preschool room seemed so ordinary. Still—like Anna—he and his cousins had done their best. They hadn't blown it this year.

Timothy was just thinking all this when Mrs. Hendricks stuck her head in the exhibit room doorway.

She looked exasperated. And she sounded exasperated when she said, "Timothy. Titus. Sarah-Jane. Come here, please. I need to talk to you."

4
THE STRAY EGG

The cousins trotted along behind Mrs. Hendricks. What was up, they wondered.

When they got to the preschool room, she told them.

She didn't sound mad. It was worse. She sounded disappointed. "Timothy, I thought we agreed that you wouldn't hide the eggs up high."

Timothy was astonished. "But we didn't!" Mrs. Hendricks pointed to a tall bookcase just inside the door. (It didn't have books for kids. Instead, it had books for parents about kids.)

"Well, then," she said. "How did that get up there?"

On the top shelf, there was something bright green peeping out at them. A plastic egg.

The cousins stared at it in disbelief.

Mrs. Hendricks was gathering up her coat and purse. She said, "I have to run out and pick up a few last-minute things for the party. Now, while I'm gone, I want you to rehide any eggs that are up too high, OK? If a preschooler spotted that one—" she pointed at the green egg, "he might climb up to get it. Some little kid could get hurt."

"But, Mrs. Hendricks!" cried Sarah-Jane. "We didn't put that one up there!"

Mrs. Hendricks looked very confused. "But you were the only ones hiding eggs for me. Listen, I have to dash. We can talk about it later. Just double-check the room, OK?"

And before the cousins could protest any further, Mrs. Hendricks was gone.

They didn't know which was worse. To really mess up. Or to do a good job and just have someone *think* you messed up.

Mrs. Hendricks had just given them a third chance. But they didn't want a third chance. They didn't think they needed a third chance.

Even so, they checked the whole room.

It was just as they suspected. The only egg-out-of-place was the green one on the high shelf.

"A stray egg," said Sarah-Jane.

But Titus asked, "How can an egg be a stray? It can't just wander off like a stray dog. Someone had to put it up there."

"Yes," said Timothy. "But who? And why?"

He brought over a little stepladder. They agreed that Timothy should be the one to get down the stray egg. There were two good reasons. First, it was his library. And second, he was the tallest. Even so, he had to stretch to reach it.

"There's something inside," he said, stepping down and giving the egg a little shake.

"Jelly beans, probably," said Titus.

"That's what's in all the other eggs," said Sarah-Jane.

"I don't know," replied Timothy doubtfully. "It doesn't sound like jelly beans."

He twisted the egg open. And the three detective-cousins crowded close to look inside.

24

INSIDE THE EGG

Inside the egg they saw a little key and a scrap of paper. Attached to the key was a tag that said:

GPL

ER

DC-7

"Now *this*," declared Titus, "is *weird*."

"The *weirdest*," agreed Sarah-Jane.

Timothy said, "And now we're *really* in trouble."

His cousins looked at him in surprise.

"Well, think about it," Timothy said. "For some crazy reason, somebody put a key in an Easter egg. Then that person put the egg up high on the grown-ups' bookcase. Usually putting stuff up high means kids aren't supposed to mess with it."

Titus said slowly, "So, if we rehide the egg like Mrs. Hendricks told us to, we could get in trouble with the person who put it there in the first place."

"Bingo," said Timothy.

Sarah-Jane said, "But if we *don't* rehide the egg, Mrs. Hendricks will think we weren't listening. And we could get in trouble with her."

"Double bingo," said Timothy.

"So now what do we do?" asked Titus. Then he answered his own question. "We have two choices. We can put the egg back where we found it. And wait around to explain it to Mrs. Hendricks. Or we can rehide the egg. And wait around to explain it to the other person."

To the cousins it sounded like they really had only one choice. And that was to sit around and wait to explain something to somebody. It sounded horrible. Besides, they were itching to get back to the World of Eggs display in the exhibit room.

In the end, they figured out a plan. They decided to rehide the egg—but only do it a little bit.

They decided to put the egg back on the same bookcase—but on a lower shelf. That way, the person who had put it there could still find it. And Mrs. Hendricks couldn't say they left an egg too high.

Usually when the cousins worked a problem out like that they felt good. But not now. It was just all too strange. Why in the world would anyone put a key in an Easter egg?

Things got even stranger when Timothy went to put the key back in the egg. The cousins saw something they hadn't noticed before. The little scrap of paper in the egg had writing on it. It said: *Lilie's gone 10—10:15. Don't take too many!!*

Titus said, "Mrs. Hendricks told us that nothing mysterious ever happens around here. But I would have to disagree with that."

"Me, too!" said Timothy and Sarah-Jane together.

Titus said, "It seems to me that somebody put the key in the egg so someone else could get it. Because—you wouldn't write a note like that to yourself."

Sarah-Jane said, "But if somebody needed to get a key, why couldn't the person just hand it to him? Or why not just leave the key in an envelope at the front desk? Why *hide* it like that?"

It was all very frustrating. They were detectives. And here was a mystery. Maybe. And they

didn't know quite what to do about it.

They read the note again. Then they put it back in the egg with the key. They put the egg on the new shelf they had picked out. It was all they could think of to do.

Sarah-Jane said, "What did it mean about the lilies being gone?"

Timothy said, "The only lilies I know about are the ones by the fountain in the main lobby."

Sarah-Jane said, "But the note said not to take too many. I didn't know people were allowed to take those lilies."

"They're not," said Timothy. "At least I don't think they are. Let's go check."

So they went to check on the lilies. But the lilies looked just fine. They stood, pot after pot, in a thick row around the fountain. It didn't look as though any were missing. It didn't even look as though any had been moved.

Timothy said, "We're forgetting about the key, you know. Why would somebody need a key to get the lilies? They're not locked up. They're just sitting out here."

The cousins slumped down on a bench to think things over.

They were thinking so hard that they almost didn't notice the telephone ringing at the main desk.

They almost didn't notice when a librarian answered it.

And they *almost* didn't notice when she called out to someone, "Lilie—telephone call for you."

7
LILIE

Timothy, Titus, and Sarah-Jane sat bolt upright and stared at one another.

Sarah-Jane gasped, "Lilie. It's a lady's name. The Lilie in the note is a *who,* not a *what.* We must have read the note wrong."

They rushed back to double-check. Sure enough, the note said *Lilie's,* not *lilies.* Sarah-Jane said, "We didn't see the apostrophe. The note doesn't mean more than one lily. It means Lilie *is.* Someone named Lilie is going to be gone for a little while."

Titus grumbled, "I think there should be a law that you can only spell names one way. Then people wouldn't get so mixed up all the time."

Sarah-Jane read the note aloud again.

" 'Lilie's gone 10-10:15. Don't take too many!!' " Then she added, "Well, if they're not taking lilies, what *are* they taking?"

Titus was still grumbling. "And who is this Lilie-person anyway? And where is she going to be gone from? The library?"

Timothy said, "We were in such a hurry to double-check the note that we didn't stay to see who came to the phone. If we had, we would know who Lilie is."

"Maybe she's still talking on the phone," suggested Sarah-Jane. (She had been known to hold some long-ish phone calls herself.)

But when they got back to the lobby, no one was on the phone.

So Timothy marched up to the front desk with Titus and Sarah-Jane right behind him.

He said to the harried-looking librarian, "Excuse me. But does someone named Lilie work here?"

The librarian was busy checking out books. She barely glanced up. "The only one I know is Lilie Johnson."

The name sounded vaguely familiar. Sud-

denly, in his mind's eye, Timothy saw a little, brass name tag. He had to test out his idea. He tried to sound casual when he asked, "She's the security guard. Right?"

"That's right."

Apparently Titus was having sudden ideas, too. Because he asked, "Can you tell us when Lilie goes on a coffee break?"

The librarian sighed a little impatiently. "The staff is not allowed to give out that information to the public. Lilie takes her break at a different time each day. For security purposes. Now, do you children have any books to check out? Because if not, you're holding up the line."

But the cousins had no intention of holding up the line.

They had to get back to the green plastic egg.

If only they weren't too late.

"Whew! Still here!" Timothy exclaimed when he checked the egg.

They all gave a huge sigh of relief. But they weren't too sure why. Something was going on. But what?

Timothy said, "What worries me is that somebody wants to know when the security guard will be out of the way. That must mean they're up to no good."

"Like stealing something, you mean?" asked Titus. "Then somebody on the library staff must be in on it. Because who else would know when Lilie takes her break?"

They didn't like the sound of that. But Timothy and Sarah-Jane knew Titus must be right.

Sarah-Jane turned the little key over in her hand. "This is a library key, isn't it? Because, see? The first letters on the tag say GPL. That must stand for Greenwood Public Library."

Timothy nodded. "Right. It does. GPL is stamped on all the books and everything."

Titus said slowly, "So—someone on the inside left a library key where someone on the outside could find it. And they just used the preschool room as a drop-off place because of the party today. They figured no one would notice an extra egg in here."

"Of all the nerve!" exclaimed Sarah-Jane. "Using a little kids' party as a cover! And look at all the trouble it got *us* into!"

"Yes, yes," said Timothy impatiently. "But we're missing the point here."

"And that is?" asked Titus.

"And that is, that the person from the outside hasn't picked up the key yet. It's still here. That means the crime probably hasn't happened yet. So we can stop it."

Sarah-Jane got so excited she bounced up and down. "I get it! All we have to do is find the security guard, Lilie, and warn her that someone is going to steal the—'' Sarah-Jane suddenly stopped her bouncing. "Steal the *what*?"

Titus picked up the key and read the tag aloud. " 'GPL. ER. DC-7.' OK, we've got the first part. 'GPL' stands for Greenwood Public Library. Now, what about 'ER'?"

"Emergency room?" guessed Timothy. "But that only makes sense for a hospital."

"Easter rabbit?" guessed Sarah-Jane. They thought about that for a moment. It seemed to go with the party and everything. But they couldn't see what the key had to do with a rabbit.

"Let's skip to the next part," said Titus. " 'DC-7.' "

"Isn't that a kind of airplane?" asked Timothy. "Maybe there's a clue hidden away in a book about airplanes." They thought about that for a moment, too. It made sense. But the idea of going through every book in the library that had something to do with airplanes . . .

"OK," said Sarah-Jane. "Let's try thinking about it another way. The key is too small to go to the front door. So it must go to something *inside* the library. What's kept locked up in a library?"

Timothy said, "The rare books. And I think there are some old maps and charts, too."

"The Xerox machine has a key, too," said Titus. But he said it doubtfully, as if he didn't really think that was the answer.

Timothy said, "The desks could be locked. Especially if the librarians keep their purses in them. And I guess at the main desk they lock up the money people pay for overdue fines. But that doesn't exactly go with the note. You wouldn't say, 'Don't take too many money.'"

Sarah-Jane sighed. "There must be something else. Those glass tables were locked. You know, the ones with the beautiful Easter eggs inside—"

The cousins stared at one another. Suddenly, the tag on the key made sense.

GPL—Greenwood Public Library

ER—Exhibit Room

DC-7—Display Case Number 7

Someone was going to steal from the *World*

of Eggs display.
   And not just any Easter eggs.
   Anna's Easter eggs.

9
SWITCHEROO

To the amazement of his cousins, Timothy began emptying his pockets.

Titus said, "Tim, it's nice that you want to get organized. But do you have to do that *NOW*?!"

"Come *on*, Tim!" cried Sarah-Jane. "We have to take the egg and go find Lilie!"

"I agree with you that we have to go tell the security guard," said Timothy calmly. He found what he was looking for and shoved the rest of the stuff back in his pockets. "But if we take the egg with us, the crooks will get suspicious. Then we'll never find out who was behind all this. And who knows? They might try it again when we're not here to stop them."

"So what do we do?" asked Titus.

Timothy grinned and said, "We set a trap. We pull an old switcheroo." And he held up the key to his bicycle lock.

Titus and Sarah-Jane instantly saw what Timothy meant. Quickly the cousins took the tag off the library key and put the tag on Timothy's key. Then they put Timothy's key back in the egg. They put the egg back on the shelf. And they put the library key in Timothy's pocket.

Titus slapped Timothy on the back and said, "Good thinking, old man! That ought to slow them down a bit."

But the cousins knew *they* couldn't afford to slow down. They had to find Lilie. Fast.

On the way, they ran into Pastor Parry again. They slowed down long enough to explain the whole thing to him. And they were glad they did. It helped to have a grown-up along when they found the security guard and told her she had to change her break time and come with them.

They got to the exhibit room just in time to see a snooty-looking lady with a big, leather

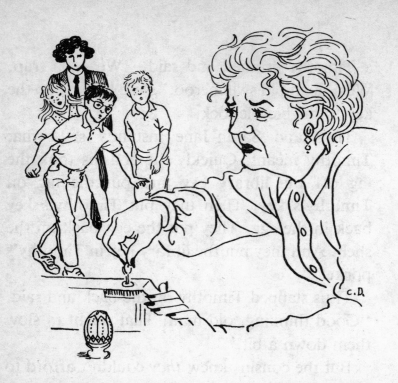

purse struggling to get Display Case 7 open. She pushed and pulled and muttered under her breath.

But for some strange reason, the key wouldn't turn in the lock.

Lilie stepped foward. "May I ask what you think you're doing?"

Caught red-handed, the woman whirled around in astonishment. "But you're—I thought—"

"I know what you thought," said Lilie. "That I'd be on my break. Come with me. We need to have a little talk."

The woman looked even more astonished when Timothy stopped her on the way out. "Excuse me," he said. "But could I please have my bicycle key back?"

"The thing that gets me," Lilie said to the cousins and Pastor Parry later, "is that the lady wasn't the least bit sorry. 'What's the big deal?' she said. 'I was going to bring them back when I was through with them.' It seems she was giving a dinner party. And she said she thought the *pysanky* would make a cute table decoration."

"*Cute*!?" snorted Timothy. (It was not one of his favorite words.) "Anna's eggs aren't *cute*! They're beautiful and special. Anna can give them to people if she wants. But no one can just go around stealing them. Who does that lady think she is, anyway?"

Titus murmured, "She's not poor in spirit like Anna. That's for sure."

Pastor Parry nodded. "And another thing's

for sure. You kids had the key and the message figured out right."

Lilie definitely agreed. "The lady had made an anonymous phone call to a library aide, who was always complaining. Anyway, she offered to leave her fifty dollars in exchange for the key. They used the Easter Egg Hunt as a cover."

The Easter Egg Hunt! The cousins looked at one another in shock.

They had forgotten all about it! Just then they heard Mrs. Hendricks calling them to come help. And then they heard another sound. A bazillion little voices, squeaky with excitement.

The preschoolers had arrived.

It was a perfectly beautiful Easter Sunday afternoon.

Yesterday at the library the Annual Preschool Easter Egg Hunt had gone off without a hitch. And Mrs. Hendricks had already signed up the T.C.D.C. to come back and help her next year.

All in all, Timothy, Titus, and Sarah-Jane couldn't remember when they'd ever had a better Easter.

But then it got even better. Pastor Parry stopped by Timothy's house. And with him was an older lady with a very kind face. Pastor Parry introduced the cousins to Anna.

"Pastor Parry told me all that you children did for me yesterday," Anna said to the cousins and their families. "He told me how you kept

the *pysanky* from being stolen. So now I will give you a little gift. Yes?"

She unwrapped a soft cloth and held out three of the most beautiful *pysanky* Easter eggs the cousins had ever seen.

Anna handed one of the eggs to Sarah-Jane and said, "Christ is risen, Sarah-Jane."

And Sarah-Jane remembered what to say as she took the egg. "He is risen indeed, Anna."

"Christ is risen, Titus."

"He is risen indeed, Anna."

"Christ is risen, Timothy."

"He is risen indeed, Anna."

And then Timothy couldn't help it. It was Easter. The Lord Jesus Christ was risen indeed. There was something he needed to add. So he threw back his head and yelled, "Yippee!!"

The End

THE TEN COMMANDMENTS MYSTERIES

When Timothy, Titus, and Sarah-Jane, the three cousins, get together the most ordinary events turn into mysteries. So they've formed the T.C.D.C. (That's the Three Cousins Detective Club.)

And while the three cousins are solving mysteries, they're also learning about the Ten Commandments and living God's way.

You'll want to solve all ten mysteries along with Sarah-Jane, Ti, and Tim:

The Mystery of the Laughing Cat—"You shall not steal." *Someone stole rare coins. Can the cousins find the thief?*

The Mystery of the Messed-up Wedding—"You shall not commit adultery." *Can the cousins find the missing wedding ring?*

The Mystery of the Gravestone Riddle—"You shall not murder." *Can the cousins solve a 100-year-old murder case?*

The Mystery of the Carousel Horse—"You shall not covet." *Why does the stranger want an old, wooden horse?*

The Mystery of the Vanishing Present—"Remember the Sabbath day and keep it holy." *Can the cousins figure out who has Grandpa's missing birthday gift?*

The Mystery of the Silver Dolphin—"You shall not give false testimony." *Who's telling the truth—and who's lying?*

The Mystery of the Tattletale Parrot—"You shall not misuse the name of the Lord your God." *What will the beautiful green parrot say next?*

The Mystery of the Second Map—"You shall have no other gods before me." *Can the cousins discover who dropped the strange map?*

The Mystery of the Double Trouble—"Honor your father and your mother." *How could Timothy be in two places at once?*

The Mystery of the Silent Idol—"You shall not make for yourself an idol." *If the idol could speak, what would it tell the cousins?*

Available at your local Christian bookstore.

David C. Cook Publishing Co., Elgin, IL 60120